GREETINGS FROM SOMEWHERE

The Mystery Across the Secret Bridge

BY HARPER PARIS • ILLUSTRATED BY MARCOS CALO

LITTLE SIMON

New York London Toronto Sydney New Delhi

LITTLE SIMON

An imprint of Simon & Schuster Children's Publishing Division • 1230 Avenue of the Americas, New York, New York 10020 • First Little Simon paperback edition March 2015 • Copyright © 2015 by Simon & Schuster, Inc. All rights reserved, including the right of reproduction in whole or in part in any form. LITTLE SIMON is a registered trademark of Simon & Schuster, Inc., and associated colophon is a trademark of Simon & Schuster, Inc. For information about special discounts for bulk purchases, please contact Simon & Schuster Special Sales at 1-866-506-1949 or business@simonandschuster.com. The Simon & Schuster Speakers Bureau can bring authors to your live event. For more information or to book an event contact the Simon & Schuster Speakers Bureau at 1-866-248-3049 or visit our website at www.simonspeakers.com. Designed by John Daly. The text of this book was set in ITC Stone Informal. Manufactured in the United States of America 0215 FFG 10 9 8 7 6 5 4 3 2 1
Library of Congress Cataloging-in-Publication Data
Paris, Harper. The mystery across the secret bridge / by Harper Paris ; illustrated by Marcos Calo. — First edition. pages cm. — (Greetings from somewhere ; #7)
Summary: While in Machu Picchu, Peru, with their parents, eight-year-old twins Ethan and Ella cross a secret bridge and discover a mysterious stone sculpture.
[1. Brothers and sisters—Fiction. 2. Twins—Fiction. 3. Incas—Fiction. 4. Antiquities—Fiction. 5. Machu Picchu Site (Peru)—Fiction. 6. Peru—Fiction. 7. Mystery and detective stories.]
I. Calo, Marcos, illustrator. II. Title. PZ7.P21748Mws 2015 [E]—dc23 2014011020
ISBN 978-1-4814-2368-7 (hc)
ISBN 978-1-4814-2367-0 (pbk)
ISBN 978-1-4814-2369-4 (eBook)

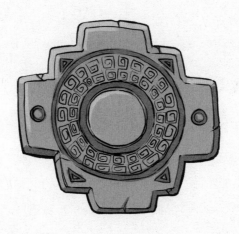

TABLE OF CONTENTS

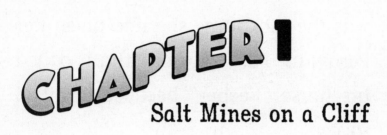

CHAPTER 1

Salt Mines on a Cliff

Ethan Briar peered over the edge of the rocky cliff. *"Whoa! That's a big drop!"* he exclaimed. The roaring river down below now looked like a skinny ribbon.

"Yeah, I believe you," said his twin sister, Ella, nervously. She kept her gaze straight ahead and clutched Butterscotch's reins. "Butterscotch" was the nickname she had given her Peruvian Paso horse. Ethan called his horse "Keeper" because he liked soccer.

Ella, Ethan, and their parents, Andy and Josephine, were horseback riding through the Sacred Valley in Peru. The guide, Fernando, led their tour group along a dirt path that went steeply uphill. Towering mountains and lush, green grass surrounded them.

The Sacred Valley was the Briars' second stop in Peru. Their first stop had been the capital city of Lima. In Lima, they explored catacombs, which were ancient passageways underground, and swam in the Pacific Ocean. It

was the same ocean they swam in when they had visited their cousins in California the year before!

The Briar family was taking a big trip around the world. Mrs. Briar was writing about their trip for the *Brookeston Times*, which was their hometown newspaper. The family had already been to Italy, France, China, Kenya, and India since leaving Brookeston several months ago.

"Kids, check it out!" Mrs. Briar said, pointing.

The twins gasped. Up ahead was a sight that was both totally awesome and confusing at the same time! Wide terraces had been carved into the side of a mountain. Along those terraces were little pools. Hundreds of white patches covered the pools, like snow.

Except that it wasn't snow.

"We have arrived at the *salineras de Maras*, or the salt mines of Maras," Fernando, the guide, explained. "The people of this area have harvested salt here since before the time of the Incas. There is natural salt water inside this mountain. The people let the salt water collect into pools. They wait for the

water to evaporate, or dry up, in the sun. What remains are those white patches of salt you see before you."

"Cool!" Ethan said. He and Ella knew about evaporation from their dad's science lessons. He was homeschooling the second graders.

"What are Incas?" Ella whispered to Mr. Briar.

"The Incas were a civilization of people who used to live here more than five hundred years ago," Mr. Briar whispered back.

"Can we walk around?" Mrs. Briar asked Fernando as she tucked her blond hair behind her ear.

"*Sí*. We will tether our horses and explore the mines on foot," Fernando replied. "We will even be able to taste some of the salt."

People from the tour group began tying their horses to posts.

As Ella tied up her horse, she noticed a little boy nearby. A blue toy snake was draped across his shoulders.

"Isn't this great, Slither?" the little boy said to his snake.

Standing next to him was a teen-aged girl. She didn't look very happy.

Ella wondered who they were. But before she could find out, it was time to begin the tour of the salt mines.

CHAPTER 2

The Temple of the Sun

The Briars spent the rest of the morning touring the salt mines. In the afternoon, they visited a nearby village. There, the twins got to meet some baby alpacas, which looked like small llamas. Ethan and Ella even helped weave some hats and scarves out of alpaca wool!

Later that day, they checked out

of their hotel in Maras and traveled to Aguas Calientes, Peru. The town's name, Aguas Calientes, meant "hot water" in Spanish, and it was known for its natural hot springs. So the Briars put on their swimsuits. The springs were warm—like Jacuzzis!

For dinner, the family went to a restaurant and ate a local dish called *pachamanca*. *Pachamanca*, or "earth pot," was a way of cooking meat and vegetables under the ground with hot stones, leaves, and dirt. For dessert, they had *picarones*, which were fried doughnuts made out of pumpkin, sweet potato, and syrup.

"Kids, it's early bedtime tonight," Mr. Briar announced when they got back to their hotel. He sank down on a cushy chair with a yawn.

Mrs. Briar skimmed through her notes. "That's right. We'll be waking up at five a.m. to take the bus to Machu Picchu."

Ethan and Ella said good night to their parents. Then they brushed their teeth, went to their room, and changed into their pajamas.

They didn't want to go to sleep right away, though.

First they admired their souvenirs from the day. Ella's included a bag of pink salt and a purple alpaca scarf. The purple dye had been made out of berries and flowers. Ethan's included a bag of white salt and a green alpaca hat. The green dye had been made out of leaves and plant stems.

Next they decided to check their

e-mail. A new message popped up on the computer screen. It was from Grandpa Harry! It had been a while since they'd heard from him.

The subject line said: THE TEMPLE OF THE SUN.

The Temple of the Sun?

Ethan pulled on his hat and Ella wrapped her scarf around her neck as they read the e-mail together.

SUBJECT: THE TEMPLE OF THE SUN

Hello, my dears! *¡Bienvenido a Peru!* (That means "welcome to Peru" in Spanish!)

Your mother tells me that your next adventure will be to explore Machu Picchu. This ancient Incan city is located on a high mountain ridge. Your grandma Lucy and I visited it many years ago. We woke up in the middle of the night to hike to the top and see the sunrise!

While you are there, be sure to check out the Temple of the Sun. Also, I seem to remember something interesting near the temple. I believe it had to do with a bird, a snake, and another animal. I know that we used rope to get to it.

You will have to find it for yourselves and report back to me. Good luck, my dears—and have fun!

Adiós y amor,

Grandpa Harry

Ethan frowned. "How are we supposed to find this thing? We don't
even know what it looks like!" he complained to Ella.

"Well, we do have *some* clues," Ella
pointed out.

She reached for her messenger bag and pulled out her purple notebook. Grandpa Harry had given it to her as a going-away present before their family left on their big trip.

She picked up a pen and wrote:

Check out the Temple of the Sun.
Find something nearby that has
to do with a bird, a snake, and
another animal.
Use rope to get to it.

CHAPTER 3

He's Gone!

"Good morning!"

Mrs. Briar stood next to the beds in the twins' room, hands on her hips. She looked excited and ready to go in her new alpaca sweater, jeans, and hiking boots.

Ella rubbed her eyes. It was still dark outside. "What time is it?" she groaned.

"It's time to go back to sleep," Ethan mumbled, pulling a pillow over his head.

Mrs. Briar glanced at her watch. "Guys, you have exactly fifteen minutes to get dressed and grab some breakfast. Otherwise, our bus to Machu Picchu will leave without us."

"Can't we just catch the next one?" Ella begged.

"Or the one after that?" came Ethan's voice from under the pillow.

"I never told you this. But Grandpa Harry and Grandma Lucy visited Machu Picchu many years ago. *They* got up before dawn so they could hike to the top and see the sunrise," Mrs. Briar said with a wink.

Ella and Ethan shared a smile. Their mom had no idea that Grandpa Harry had already mentioned all this in his e-mail!

"Hey, what's so funny?" Mrs. Briar asked.

"Nothing, Mom. We'll get up now," said Ella.

"Bet I can get dressed faster than you!" Ethan challenged as he jumped out of bed.

"No way!" Ella yelled.

A short while later, the Briar family was on the bus to Machu Picchu. Along the way, Mr. Briar gave the

twins a brief lesson on the historic site. He explained that Machu Picchu had likely been built as an estate for one of the Incan emperors. He added that it was often called the "Lost City of the Incas."

The bus chugged slowly up the mountain road. The twins gazed out the window. In the distance, dawn was beginning to break. The sky was streaked with pinks and golds.

"Can you believe we're almost eight thousand feet in the air?" Mrs. Briar remarked.

"Wow!" said Ella. No wonder it felt like they were in the clouds.

A few minutes later, the bus arrived at the entrance to Machu Picchu, and everyone got off.

"This . . . is . . . incredible!" Mr. Briar gushed.

Mrs. Briar began snapping pictures with her camera.

The twins looked from left to right to take in the sweeping view. Before them was a vast village of stone buildings that had been built into the mountainside. A gray mist blanketed

the landscape. They felt as though they had stepped into a long-ago time. And not just that—but a long-ago time in the *clouds*!

Ethan tried to count the number of buildings, then gave up. There had to be at least a hundred— maybe even two hundred.

"How are we going to find Grandpa Harry's temple?" he asked Ella.

"It won't be easy," Ella replied with a worried look.

Just then, someone yelled: *"He's gone!"*

CHAPTER 4

New Friends

The twins turned around. A little boy was talking to his dad. He looked upset.

"Hey, that's the boy from yesterday!" Ella said to Ethan.

Ethan nodded.

The mother of the family glanced up and waved to the Briars.

"Hello! You were in our tour group

at the salt mines," she called out.
"We're the Novaks. This is our son,
Dylan, and our daughter, Deanna."

Mrs. Briar smiled and introduced
her family.

Dylan tugged on Mrs. Novak's jacket. *"Mom!* This is an *emergency!* We have to find him *now!"*

"Find who?" Ethan asked Dylan curiously.

"Slither. He's the fiercest anaconda in the whole wide world!" Dylan cried out.

"We just returned from the Temple of the Sun. Dylan thinks he lost his toy snake there," Mr. Novak explained to the Briars.

The Temple of the Sun? Ella elbowed Ethan. He elbowed her back.

"We have to go back there right this second!" Dylan told his parents.

"We can't do that, honey. We're going to the museum now," Mrs. Novak said patiently. "Maybe later."

"Museum? What museum?" asked Mrs. Briar.

"There is a museum with exhibits about the history of Machu Picchu," Mr. Novak replied. "I teach history at Addison College," he added.

Mr. Briar beamed. "Really? I teach history at Brookeston University!"

"You should come to the museum with us!" Mrs. Novak suggested. "Hey, I have a good idea. Deanna, why don't you take your brother back to the Temple of the Sun to look for his snake? We can meet back here at ten o'clock."

"Really, Mom? Do I have to?" Deanna complained.

Ella elbowed Ethan again. He turned to their parents.

"Can we go with Deanna and Dylan? Please?" Ethan begged.

"Please?" Ella echoed.

"Deanna is sixteen. She's very responsible. And she knows the way to the temple and back because we were just there," said Mrs. Novak.

Mr. Briar pushed his glasses up on his nose. "Well . . . I don't see why not," he said after a moment.

Mrs. Briar nodded. "You must stay with Deanna the whole time. Okay, kids?"

Ethan and Ella grinned at each other.

Temple of the Sun, here we come! Ethan thought excitedly.

CHAPTER 5

Snake Search

Deanna, Dylan, and the twins started for the Temple of the Sun. Bushy trees and moss-covered rocks lined the craggy path. The early-morning sun lit up the nearby mountains.

"So when was the last time you saw your snake?" Ella asked Dylan.

"I was playing with it at the sunny temple place," replied Dylan.

Ella pulled her purple notebook out of her bag. She flipped it open to a blank page and wrote:

> Dylan's blue snake is missing.
> Last seen at the Temple of
> the Sun.

Deanna peeked over Ella's shoulder. "What are you doing?" she asked.

"I like to take notes whenever there's a mystery to solve," Ella explained.

Dylan perked up. "Mystery? Wow, are you, like, superhero detectives?"

Ella grinned. "Not exactly. But when we were in Paris, France, we found a stolen painting. And when we were in Mumbai, India, we solved a mystery about spices."

"We've solved mysteries in Italy, China, Kenya, and back home in Brookeston, too," Ethan added.

"Cool! Can you solve the mystery of my snake?" Dylan asked eagerly.

"We're already on the case!" said Ella.

The four of them continued
down the path. They passed
a cluster of stone buildings.

Up close, Ethan could
see how huge and heavy
the stones were.

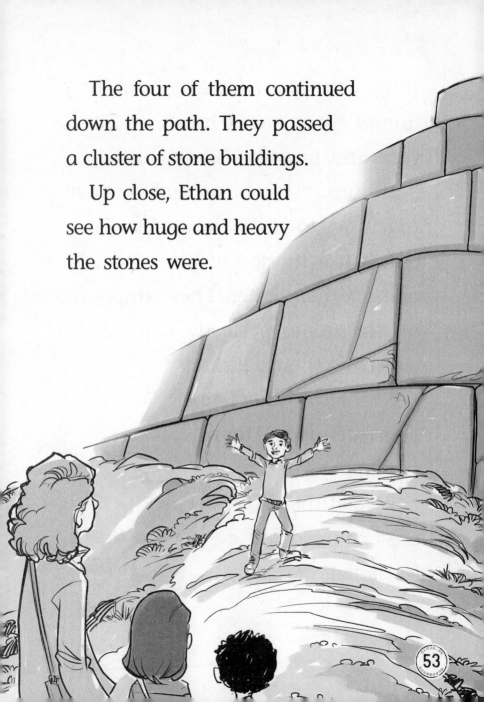

During the bus ride, Mr. Briar had taught them about Incan architecture and how the Incas built their buildings. The Incas didn't have machines to carry the stones. They didn't use mortar to glue them to one another, either. They simply fit all the stones perfectly together to construct their buildings.

The Incas must have been really smart, Ethan thought.

Beyond the cluster of stone buildings, a few llamas grazed by

the side of the path. They were brown
and white and way bigger than alpacas.

"Hi, llamas! Do you guys live here?"
Ella called out.

The llamas blinked at her.

Deanna reached into her purse and

pulled out an apple. She held it out to the llamas.

The llamas made an excited humming sound as they moved closer to Deanna. They jostled one another to get to the apple first. Then one of them opened its mouth and spat at another one!

"Ew!" Deanna cried out. She stuffed the apple back in her

pocket. "Let's get out of here before they spit on *us!*"

"Good idea!" Ethan said with a laugh.

The four of them hurried down the path. Just as they turned a corner, Dylan began jumping up and down.

"There's the Temple of the Sun!" he shouted.

CHAPTER 6

Hidden Steps

The Temple of the Sun was a large stone building with a tower, lots of small windows, and no roof. Inside one of the rooms was a long, flat rock that looked like a bed. Tourists wandered in and out and snapped pictures.

"I wonder why it's called the Temple of the Sun," Ethan said as they walked up to it.

"Actually, our dad told us why," began Deanna. "It turns out that the Incas built this temple in a special way. On the longest day of the year, the sun shines through one of the windows and lights up that big rock."

"Cool!" Ella exclaimed. No wonder Grandpa Harry had wanted them to see it!

Dylan stood on his tiptoes and peered through a window. "Slither, where are you?" he called out.

"If we want to find Slither, we should probably retrace your steps," Ethan suggested.

"Huh? What does that mean?" asked Dylan.

"That means you should try to remember exactly where you were before. Then we'll look for Slither in all those places," Ella explained.

"Oh, okay!" Dylan put his hands on his hips and scrunched up his face. "Well . . . first, I went all around the temple with my mom and dad and Deanna. Then I sat under that leafy tree and ate some bunny crackers," he

said, pointing. "Then I played in that grassy part over there," he added, pointing in a different direction.

Ella wrote all this down in her notebook. "Got it. Okay, let's get started!"

She, Ethan, Dylan, and Deanna circled the temple once, twice, then three times. There was no sign of Slither.

Next they looked under the leafy tree. They found a couple of bunny crackers, but no Slither.

Finally, they went over to the grassy area. Still no Slither.

"Somebody stole him!" Dylan wailed. "He's gone forever!"

"Wait!" Ella got down on her hands and knees. She crawled through the tall, thick grass in search of Slither.

She was just about to give up when she saw a flash of blue. It was Slither, hidden in the grass!

Ella picked up the snake and rose to her feet. Just then the sun peeked out from behind a cloud and lit up a patch of wildflowers nearby.

On the other side of the flowers was a set of stone steps.

CHAPTER 7

A Secret Bridge

Dylan, Deanna, and Ethan rushed up to Ella. Ella handed Slither to Dylan.

"You found him!" Dylan said, hugging Slither.

"I found something else, too!" Ella said, pointing to the stone steps.

Ethan walked over to the top of the steps. They sloped down a gentle cliff and disappeared into the mist.

Steps to nowhere, Ethan thought.

He squatted down and peered over the edge. Actually, the steps *did* lead somewhere. They curled around the side of the cliff and went down pretty far.

Ella knelt down next to Ethan. "Grandpa Harry wanted us to

find something near the Temple of Sun that had to do with a snake, a bird, and another animal," she said slowly. "Do you think this is the way to get there?"

"Maybe," Ethan replied.

"What are you two talking about?" Deanna asked.

Ethan told Deanna and Dylan about Grandpa Harry's e-mail. "Ella and I are going to check it out. You guys can wait here if you want."

Deanna shook her head. "No way. We're coming with you. I promised your parents I would look after you."

"Slither, we're going on an adventure!" Dylan said happily. They started down the steps. Ella took a quick peek in her notebook. "Grandpa Harry told us that he and Grandma Lucy used rope to get to this special place," she reminded Ethan.

"Maybe they used rope to climb up a mountain," Deanna suggested.

"Or maybe they used rope to swing from tree to tree like monkeys!" Dylan said, giggling.

The four of them continued walking down the stairs. Thick mist swirled around them. Ella wondered where the sun had gone.

After a while, they reached the bottom of the steps. Before them was a narrow bridge that stretched into the mist. It was made of wooden slats and rope.

"Rope!" the twins said together.

Ella hesitated. It didn't look very safe. But she knew Grandpa Harry would never lead them into danger.

They began crossing the bridge. Ethan led the way, and Deanna brought up the rear. The wooden slats wobbled beneath their feet. The rope railings barely kept them steady. And the mist made it hard to see.

Ella glanced over the side—and gulped. The valley below was barely visible. They were up *very* high on a *very* old bridge. *Be brave*, she told herself.

"Eth—Ethan. I'm not sure about this," she stammered.

Ethan thought for a moment. He could tell everyone was nervous.

"What's a snake's favorite class in school?" he asked.

"What?" asked Dylan, confused.

"*Hiss*-tory!" replied Ethan.

Dylan and Ella laughed. Deanna cracked a smile.

"What color socks does a bear wear?" Ethan went on.

"What color?" asked Ella.

"He doesn't wear socks because he has bare feet," said Ethan. "Get it? Like, *bear* feet."

Ethan told several more jokes. Before long, they had reached the other side.

Ethan stepped off the bridge and looked around. There was no sign of what Grandpa Harry had told them about—just trees, rocks, and grass. He tried to hide his disappointment.

Ella came up to him. "Maybe this was the wrong way," she said quietly.

A cry sounded from above. The twins lifted their faces to the sky. A

massive black bird circled in the air.

The bird swooped down toward the ground. It landed on top of a big rock formation behind a row of trees.

Except . . . it wasn't just *any* rock formation. It looked like a cave!

CHAPTER 8

The Tree of Life

The bird perched on top of the cave entrance and fixed its beady eyes on the foursome.

"Is it going to eat us?" Dylan asked nervously.

"Of course not!" Deanna replied, although she didn't sound very sure.

Ethan reached into his pocket and pulled out his gold coin. Grandpa

Harry had given it to him as a going-away present. It had a hawk on one side and a globe on the other.

That bird up there doesn't look like a hawk. It must be something else, Ethan thought.

"Maybe it wants us to go into the cave," Ella guessed.

The bird gave another screech, flew off in the direction of the bridge, and vanished into the mist.

Ethan hurried up to the cave entrance and peered inside. "Hello?" he shouted.

Hellooooo? his voice echoed back.

He turned his body sideways and inched through the narrow opening. The other three did the same. The air in the cave was cool and smelled like clay. A *drip, drip* sound came from somewhere within.

"I can't see anything. Can you?"
Ella asked her brother.

"Too dark," Ethan replied.

Deanna held up her cell phone.
"This might help," she said, touching
the screen.

A pale light flickered on. It lit up a small section of the rocky cave floor.

Deanna swung the phone around in a slow arc. It lit up more of the floor and several rocky walls. A thin trickle of water dripped from the ceiling.

Then she swung the phone to the middle of the cave.

Ella gasped. So did Ethan.

There, in the center, stood a tall stone sculpture.

The sculpture was made up of three creatures: a bird, some kind of wildcat, and a snake. The bird looked like the one they had just seen outside the cave.

89

Ella turned to Ethan. "We found it!" she said excitedly.

Ethan grinned and nodded. "Yeah! But what is that animal? Is it a tiger?"

"Maybe it's a panther," Deanna guessed.

"Maybe it's a mountain lion. *Roar!*" Dylan growled.

"It's a puma," a voice came from behind them.

Ella screamed. Dylan screamed, too. Deanna grabbed her brother and held him close.

"Who's there?" Ethan demanded.

A flashlight clicked on. A bright light fell across the cave.

A gray-haired man stood just inside the cave entrance. Who was he?

The man stepped forward. Ethan and the others stepped back.

Then Ella noticed a badge on his khaki shirt. The badge said: HECTOR RUIZ, VOLUNTEER, MACHU PICCHU.

Deanna noticed it, too. "You work here?" she asked him.

"Yes! My name is Hector. I'm one of the volunteers here at Machu Picchu," he replied. "I am so sorry for scaring you children. I came by to check on this sculpture. It is a very valuable artifact of the Inca civilization."

"That means it's something that the Incas left behind," Deanna whispered to the group.

"Our grandpa Harry is a famous archaeologist. He's studied lots and lots of artifacts. He's the one who told us to find this sculpture," Ella said to Hector.

Hector's eyes twinkled. "Is your grandfather Harry Robinson, by any chance?"

"You know Grandpa Harry?" asked Ethan, surprised.

"Yes, from long ago," Hector replied. "I'm glad he led you to this sculpture. Did he tell you that it represents the Tree of Life?"

Ella shook her head. "No. What's that?"

"The 'Tree of Life' symbolizes how the Incas viewed the world," Hector explained. "See the snake? It is at the bottom since snakes are closest to the earth. The puma is in the middle. And this bird, which is the condor, is at the very top. Birds are closest to the sky."

The four kids listened, fascinated.

"The Tree of Life is also displayed in this way," Hector said, pulling a charm from his pocket. "You are lucky to have found the secret bridge that leads to this cave. Not many people know about it," Hector added.

"We like to find secret stuff," said Ethan with a smile.

"We're superhero detectives!" Dylan piped up.

Everyone laughed.

CHAPTER 9

Superhero Detectives!

It was midmorning when Hector walked the kids back over the rickety wood and rope bridge. Somehow, the crossing didn't seem quite so scary this time. Maybe it was Hector's presence. Or maybe it was the sun shining brightly in the sky.

"Do you know how to get back to where your parents are waiting for you?" Hector asked when they had reached the other side.

"No problem! We'll just retrace our steps," Ella replied.

They thanked Hector and said good-bye. Then they hurried up the stone steps and found the path toward the Temple of the Sun.

They passed the Temple of the Sun . . . then the grazing llamas . . . then the cluster of stone buildings. Ethan glanced nervously at his watch. They were supposed to meet their parents at the main entrance in just a few minutes. Would they make it in time?

The foursome reached the entrance exactly at ten. Their parents arrived a few minutes later.

"I'm sorry we kept you waiting. It was hard to tear ourselves away from the wonderful museum!" Mrs. Briar apologized.

"I hope you kids had fun. We can't wait to hear all about your adventures," Mr. Briar added.

"Did you find your snake?" Mrs. Novak asked Dylan.

Dylan held up Slither. "Yeah! And we found another snake, too. And a condor. And a puma."

"They weren't real," Ella added quickly.

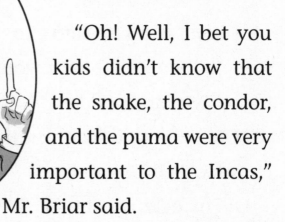

"Oh! Well, I bet you kids didn't know that the snake, the condor, and the puma were very important to the Incas," Mr. Briar said.

Mr. Novak spoke up. "Yes, they represent the three levels in the Tree of Life."

"That's really interesting," Ethan said, elbowing Ella.

"We already knew that because we're superhero detectives!" Dylan burst out. "We solved the mystery of the missing Slither. Then we found a secret bridge. Then a magical bird told us to go into a cave to find the treasure!"

"That's very nice, honey," Mrs. Novak said, patting Dylan on the head. "Okay, so, who's ready for another hike?"

The twins winked at Deanna, and Deanna winked back.

"I guess this vacation isn't so boring, after all," Deanna told them with a smile. "Thanks, guys."

"You're welcome!" said Ella.

Just then, Ethan heard a familiar-sounding cry from above. He shielded his eyes from the sun. It was the black bird from before!

"Thanks for helping us find Grandpa Harry's treasure," Ethan whispered.

The bird gave a shriek and disappeared into the clouds.

GLOSSARY

Adiós = Good-bye

Amor = Love

Bienvenido a Peru = Welcome to Peru

Salineras de Maras = Salt mines of Maras

Sí = Yes

"That girl's going to fall off the bridge!" Ella Briar shouted.

Her twin brother, Ethan, looked up. The Sydney Harbor Bridge gleamed against the bright blue sky.

At the top of the massive bridge was a girl peering over the side. How did she get all the way up there?

And then Ethan saw that there were other people with her. Lots of other people.

"It's okay, kids. You can actually climb to the top of the bridge," their father, Andrew, explained.

"The view is supposed to be

spectacular!" their mother, Josephine, added.

"Wow!" Ella gazed out at the skyline of downtown Sydney and at the sailboats that dotted the harbor. The view from the top of the bridge probably was great. Still, she couldn't imagine being up that high. She'd had enough of high places after Machu Picchu!

Machu Picchu was an ancient Incan city in Peru that was thousands of feet in the air. The Briars had spent time there before flying to Australia. Australia was the seventh stop on their trip around the world. Mrs. Briar was a travel writer.

She was writing about their adventures for their hometown newspaper, the *Brookeston Times*.

The twins were excited to be in Australia. It was beautiful and warm, plus everyone spoke English, which meant that it was easy to communicate. Best of all, they were driving up the coast tomorrow to visit their aunt Julia, their uncle Owen, and their cousin Harry.

"Who's hungry for some Balmain bugs?" Mr. Briar called out.

"Bugs?" Ethan and Ella gasped in horror.

Mr. Briar laughed. "They're not actually bugs. They're a kind of lobster. I thought we'd check out a seafood restaurant for lunch."

"And after lunch, we're going there." Mrs. Briar pointed to a white building that jutted out into the bay.

Ethan squinted. The building looked like a row of stegosaurus spikes. "What is it?"

"It's the Sydney Opera House. We'll do a backstage tour and then stay for the opera," replied Mrs. Briar.

"What about the aquarium?" asked Ella. "Hannah's family went there last summer. She said it was awesome!" Hannah was Ella's best friend back in Brookeston.

"I wish we could fit that in. But we won't have time today. And we're leaving Sydney first thing tomorrow morning," said Mrs. Briar.

Ella pouted. Ethan was disappointed, too. He had really wanted to experience some real live sea creatures while they were in Australia! Maybe there would be another chance for that.

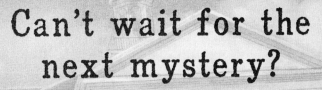

Can't wait for the next mystery?

Find activities, series info, and more.

GREETINGSFROMSOMEWHEREBOOKS.COM

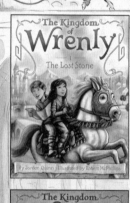
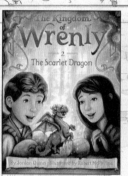

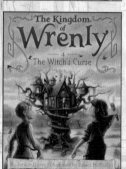
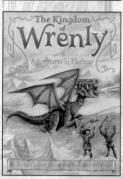